It's a unicorn! His name is Unicornio, and ne wants to bring some Unicorn Flowers home to his *mami*. Unicorn Flowers look just like Unicornio's horn. Can you see them?

Unicornio has to ride the rainbow home so he can give the flowers to his *mami*. But the rainbow is going away. We have to help Unicornio get to the rainbow. Who do we ask for help when we don't know which way to go? Map!

Map says that we'll need to go past the Dragon's Cave and over the Troll Bridge to get to the rainbow. Let's go!

We're on our way to the Dragon's Cave. Look! It's Boots and Tico, playing football. But here comes a big rain cloud. They can't play football in the rain!

I know! Isa's bag has lots of special seeds. Which special flower can block out the rain?

¡Sí! Umbrella Flowers can block the rain. Good thinking!
Let's sprinkle the seeds on the football field. Now, to make the
Umbrella Flowers grow, say *"¡Crezcan, flores!"*

¡Fantástico! The Umbrella Flowers blocked the rain so Boots and Tico can keep playing football. Now we need to find the Dragon's Cave! Can you see it?

Uh-oh! The dragon is blocking the path. We've got to get past the dragon so Unicornio can get home to his *mami*. My friend Mei has read lots of dragon stories. Maybe she can help us get past the dragon. Can you see Mei?

Mei says that dragons love a special dragon dance. If we do the dance, the dragon will get out of our way!

Let's do the dragon dance! First stomp your feet, then flap your arms, and then roar! Look! The dragon is letting us pass!

Oh, no! On the way to the Troll Bridge, Swiper swiped the Unicorn Flowers and threw them into the bushes. We've got to find the flowers so Unicornio can give them to his *mami.* Can you see the flowers?

You found the flowers! *¡Gracias!*
Come on! Let's take Unicornio to the end of the rainbow so he can get home to his *mami!*

We made it to the Troll Bridge! But the Grumpy Old Troll won't let us cross unless we solve his riddle! Will you help us solve the riddle? Great! He's asking us: "What grows from seeds when the rain showers?"

Flowers! You solved the riddle! The Grumpy Old Troll really likes purple flowers. Can you see any purple flower seeds in Isa's bag? Great! Now say *"crezcan flores"* to make them grow!

The Grumpy Old Troll loves the purple flowers!
We've got to get Unicornio to the rainbow. Can you see a rainbow? There it is – way up there! How are we going to get up that high?

Isa has some Beanstalk Flower seeds in her bag. Can you see the Beanstalk Flower seeds? Great! What do we say to get the flowers to grow? Yeah! *¡Crezcan, flores!*

It worked! We just have to climb up the Beanstalk Flowers to reach the rainbow! But some leaves are too small for Unicornio to climb! He needs our help to find leaves big enough for him to climb on. Let's find all the big leaves and show Unicornio the way to the top of the beanstalk.

Oh, no! Isa fell through the rainbow! We have to rescue her and catch the Unicorn Flowers!

We rescued Isa, crossed the rainbow, and made it to Unicorn Forest. Can you see *Mami* Unicorn?

Unicornio is so happy to see his *mami*. He made her a Unicorn Flower necklace. How sweet!

We helped Unicornio bring Unicorn Flowers to his *mami*! What a magical day! We did it!